Contents

The Big Zero   5

A Bunch of Weirdos   16

Just Act Naturally   26

Mummy Mayhem   37

Reading Ladder

The Big Zero

Welcome to The Land of Sand, where the Mummy family is having breakfast in their lovely pyramid by the river. At least, that's what they're supposed to be doing. But the day seems to have begun rather badly . . .

5

'Oh, no!' gasped Daddy Mummy suddenly. He was sitting at the table with the newspaper and the morning post laid out in front of him.

This is awful!

'Well, really!' said Mummy Mummy. 'If that's all the thanks I get for slaving over a hot stove, you can cook your own breakfast in future!'

'He does have a point, Mum,' said Tut.
'You burnt the toast.'

Ugh, gross!

'And these eggs are as hard as rocks,'
said Sis, tapping them.

Eggstraordinary!

'What do you expect?' said Mummy
Mummy. 'I was distracted because you two kids
were arguing so much. It was
chaos in here!'

No need to cry
over spilt milk!

'SHE started it,' Tut muttered, poking his sister in the side.

'I didn't,' squeaked Sis, poking him right back. 'HE did . . . '

Soon they were yelling at each other, and Mummy Mummy was yelling at them. The Mummy Puss crept off to hide in his tomb.

'QUIET!' Daddy Mummy shouted at last, and silence fell. 'I was actually talking about our bank statement, dear, not your cooking.'

'Bank statement?' said Mummy Mummy. 'What's wrong with it?'

'Er . . . there's nothing in our bank account,' said Daddy Mummy. 'Zip. Zilch. The Big Zero. We have NO money. In short, we're DEAD broke.'

Look!

'Who cares?' said Tut. 'It doesn't make any difference, does it?'

'Especially as we don't get much pocket money anyway,' said Sis.

'You won't be getting any at all from now on,' said Daddy Mummy. 'There won't be any more treats either, no sweets or comics or toys . . .'

You can't do that!

How will we survive?

'But . . . that's cruelty to children!' squealed Tut and Sis together.

'On the contrary,' said Mummy Mummy. 'It will do you good.'

'And you'll have to stop shopping, dear,' said Daddy Mummy.

'WHAT?' squealed Mummy Mummy, horrified. 'But . . . but I can't!'

'You don't have any choice,' said Daddy Mummy. 'I mean, I'm not happy about all this myself. I can't go snowboarding with my pals now.'

'There must be something we can do!' said Mummy Mummy.

'Hey, I know!' said Tut. 'We could sell stuff we don't want.'

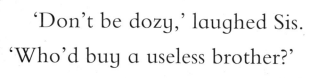

'Don't be dozy,' laughed Sis. 'Who'd buy a useless brother?'

'Hang on a second,' said Daddy Mummy.
He was staring at the newspaper and
sounded excited. 'I've got a better idea. Look
at this . . .'

He pointed to a large advertisement on the newspaper's front page.

'I think we should give it a shot,' said
Daddy Mummy. 'We've got nothing to lose,
have we? We might even turn out to be TV
stars!'

He was right, of course. But not quite in
the way he imagined . . .

A Bunch of Weirdos

Mummy Mummy called the phone number in the advertisement, and they were invited to come to the office of Sphinx TV that same afternoon. It was a colossal building in Memphis, and they were rather impressed.

'Whoa, a whole wall of TV screens,' said Tut. 'That is so cool.'

'Hey, look!' Sis hissed. 'It's the presenter from Mummy Mania!'

The Mummy kids and Daddy Mummy wanted to stop for autographs, but the nice Mummy at reception said they were expected upstairs. And when they got out of the lift, they were met by another smiling Mummy.

'Great to meet you!' he said, shaking their hands. 'I'm the Producer of *Fabulous Families!*, the show you've come to audition for today.'

'Audition?' said Daddy Mummy. 'Nobody mentioned an audition.'

Thanks for coming along.

But the Producer didn't listen. He took them to a room where there were lots of TV company Mummies – and a couple of other families too.

'Huh, what a bunch of weirdos they are,' Tut muttered. 'Yeah, they're even uglier than you,' Sis whispered. Tut stuck his tongue out at her, and Mummy Mummy gave them both a Don't-Be-So-Rude glare. But she didn't get a chance to tell them off.

Weird!

'OK, the idea of *Fabulous Families* is very
simple,' the Producer said. 'We'll put cameras
in the homes of the families we choose and
film them day and night.' Mummy Mummy
and Daddy Mummy looked at each other,
eyes wide. 'And the winners will be the
family our viewers think is the best! So,
Mr and Mrs Frankenstein, why should you
be on the show?'

'Well, we're a very loving family,' said Mr Frankenstein, smiling at his wife and children, who smiled lovingly back. 'I suppose that's because my wife and I have always felt that we were made for each other . . .'

'Ugh, yuck!' Sis murmured. 'I think I'm going to be sick.'

'Wow, they're even weirder than I thought,' Tut muttered.

Then it was the turn of the other family to talk about themselves.

Mr and Mrs Dracula and their kids had lots of hobbies. 'We like to have something we can get our teeth into . . .' said the Count.

'And for us, it was love at first bite.'

'Talk about tough competition,' said Daddy Mummy. 'For heaven's sake, he likes housework!'

'You're right,' said Mummy Mummy. 'It's just not natural.'

'That's terrific, Mr and Mrs Dracula,' the Producer was saying.

'Now, what about you, Mr and Mrs, er . . . Mummy? What have you got to say?'

You tell them dear.

Umm . . . er . . . umm . . .

Daddy Mummy opened his mouth to speak, his eyes wild with panic. Then one of the TV company Mummies whispered in the Producer's ear.

'Ah, not to worry,' the Producer said. 'No one else has applied, and as we only need three families, you're all in. So . . . the best of luck to you!'

'Er . . . thanks!' said Daddy Mummy. Somehow he couldn't help thinking they were going to need as much luck as they could get . . .

We have to have them.

polish,
polish

Just Act Naturally

As soon as they got home,
Mummy Mummy and
Daddy Mummy raced round
frantically tidying up the
pyramid. They hoovered and
dusted and cleaned everywhere
– and then they turned their
attention to Tut and Sis.

'Right, you two,' said Mummy
Mummy sternly. 'I'll sort you
out some clean bandages, and
while I'm doing that you can
both tidy your tombs.'

clean,
clean

Argh!

'But I don't want to,' Sis whined. 'I like my tomb the way it is.'

'Me too,' said Tut. 'It took me centuries to make it that messy!'

'Well hard luck,' said Daddy Mummy. 'You've got till tea-time to make sure your tombs are spotless. Oh, and one more thing. Once the cameras start rolling, you'll have to be on your very best behaviour.'

Tut and Sis turned to look at each other . . . and smirked.

In your dreams, Dad!

'No, I mean it,' said Daddy Mummy.
'Come on, kids, this is important. Just think
how much pocket money you might get if
we win that prize.'

Er . . . exactly how much
are we talking about?

'Hey, I hope you're not expecting us to
behave like those other kids,' said Sis. 'In fact,
I don't think they're really kids at all –
they're robots.'

'Actually, you'll do as you're told for once,' said Mummy Mummy. 'And NO misbehaving allowed. We'll be keeping an eye on you . . .'

Tut and Sis scowled at her, then trudged off to their tombs. A little while later somebody knocked on the pyramid door . . .

It was the Producer, and with him was a crew of Mummy technicians.

'Hi there!' said the Producer. 'It won't take us long to set things up . . .' The technicians swarmed in and got busy. 'The cameras are automatic,' said the Producer, 'so we don't need to be here. OK, I think that does it. Wait for the green light to go on . . . and remember, just act naturally.'

'Right, act naturally,' muttered Daddy Mummy as he shut the door. He waited for a few seconds . . . and then suddenly the green light flicked on!

'Yikes . . . hi, everybody!' squeaked Daddy Mummy. They all stood stiffly in front of a camera, and smiled very . . . stiffly.

Hel-lo ever-y-one . . .

'We're the Mummy family. This is my lovely wife, and these are our lovely children, and here we are in our, er . . . lovely home, of course. Isn't it time for supper, dear?'

'Why, yes, dear,' trilled Mummy Mummy. 'But I think it's your turn to cook. I'd love to spend some real quality time with our darling children.'

'Super!' said Daddy Mummy. 'What a, er . . . lovely idea!'

That evening, Daddy Mummy and Mummy Mummy were very posh, very patient, and sickeningly nice to each other and the kids. They didn't shout or lose their temper. But they did watch Tut and Sis constantly.

The Mummy kids had to behave and keep smiling for the whole of the next day . . .

and the day after that . . .

GRIMACE!

and the day after that.

It nearly drove them mad. Even worse, they had to watch the other two families on TV all the time.

Aren't the Frankensteins nice?

'I can't stand much more of this,' Tut muttered at last.

'Neither can I,' said Sis.

Suddenly the green light went off, and there was a knock on the door . . .

Mummy Mayhem

It was the Producer, and he didn't seem very happy.

Mummy Mummy invited him in for tea and Mummy cake, but he said he couldn't stay.

Can't stop.

'There's been a change of plan,' he said. 'Er . . . things haven't been going too well today, so we've decided not to keep the cameras rolling tonight. We'll put them back on tomorrow and see how it goes. Bye!'

Then he jumped into his car and roared off back to Memphis.

'Oh no, that must mean we're not doing anywhere near as well as the other families,' moaned Daddy Mummy. 'What should we do now?'

'I don't know about you, but first I'm going to relax,' said Mummy Mummy. 'And then tomorrow we'll just have to try a lot harder . . .'

'Did you hear that?' said Sis when their parents had gone.

'Yeah, what a nightmare!' Tut muttered. 'No amount of money is worth this kind of torture. I'd like us to lose as quickly as possible!'

'And that's bound to happen if everybody sees what we're really like . . .' said Sis. She nodded at a camera. 'So why don't we show them?'

Tut smiled, and they sidled over to look at the camera. They fiddled with it for a while, and the green light came on once more. They covered the light with an old tea towel, but made sure the lens wasn't blocked.

'There you are,' said Tut. 'Mum and Dad won't know it's on . . .'

'OK then,' said Sis, grinning. 'Let's go make some mischief!'

They want the Mummies, we'll give them the Mummies . . .

And so began the most famous night of TV in the history of The Land of Sand. They didn't just make mischief — they made Mummy mayhem.

They didn't do what they were told, they argued, they misbehaved in every way they knew how. Mummy Mummy and Daddy Mummy did lots of yelling, of course . . . but the four of them had some fun together too, the way they usually did. The cameras caught absolutely everything.

And in the morning, when they were doing some hasty tidying up, Mummy Mummy and Daddy Mummy got rather a nasty shock.

'Eeek!' squealed Daddy Mummy. 'The green light's on!'

'Oh no,' moaned Mummy Mummy. 'You don't mean . . .'

Tut and Sis giggled. Mummy Mummy and Daddy Mummy whirled round to glare at them . . . but there was a loud knocking on the door.

It was the Producer again, and this time he looked very happy indeed. Behind him were hundreds of journalists and screaming Mummy fans.

'Thank you so much for putting the cameras back on,' said the Producer. 'It was the funniest TV show I've ever seen. You're going to be megastars!'

'What, US?' said Mummy Mummy and Daddy Mummy together.

It turned out that everyone had thought all three Fabulous Families were DEAD boring – until the Mummies had shown the viewers what they were really like. Which just happened to be like most families . . .

Mummy Mummy and Daddy Mummy forgave the Mummy kids for what they'd done . . . and that enormous cash prize came in very handy!

Although it didn't seem to stop them being just as crazy as ever . . .

But then we wouldn't want that, would we?

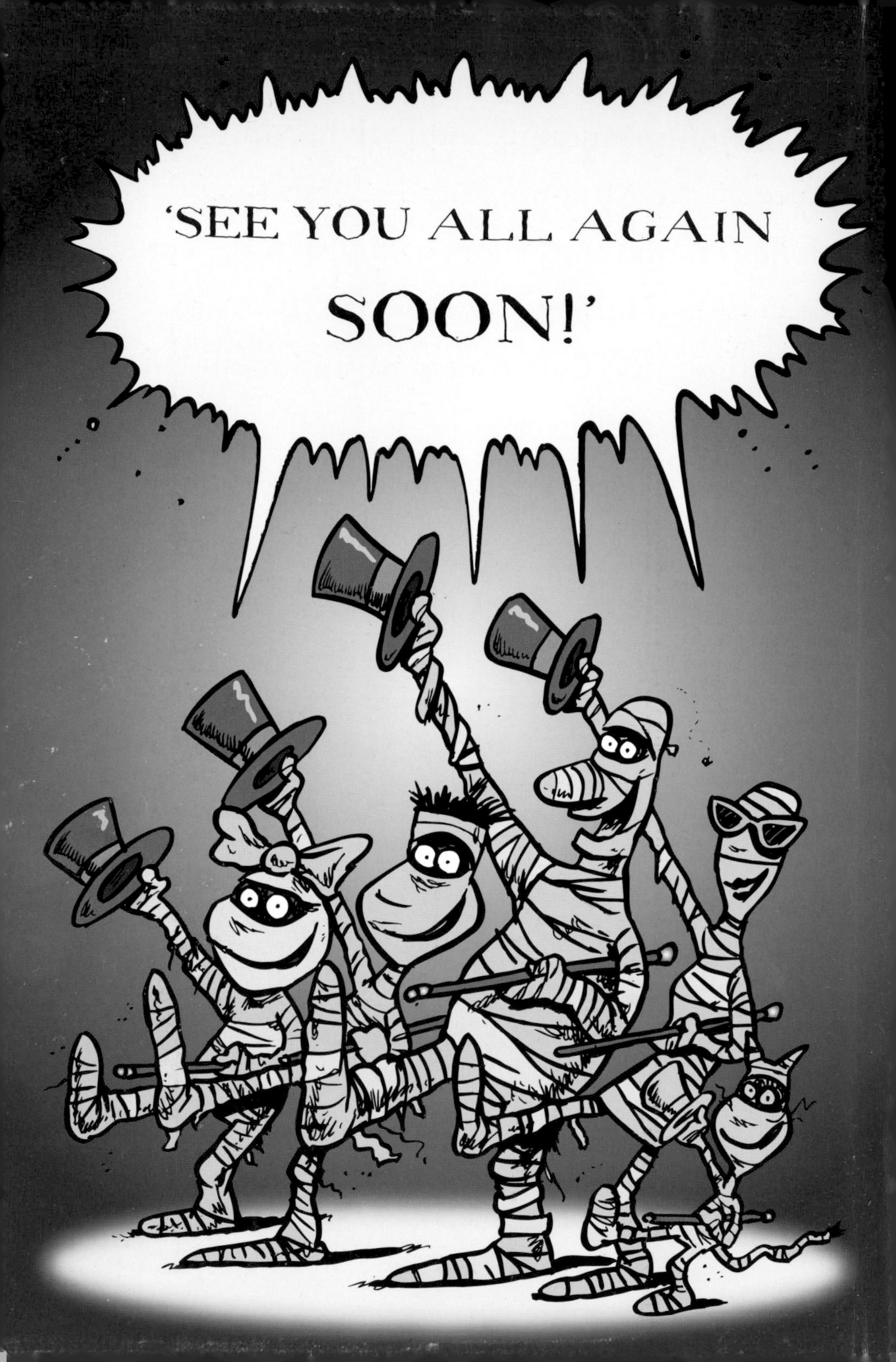
'SEE YOU ALL AGAIN SOON!'